BATMAN

FROSTBITE

by Michael Anthony Steele
Illustrated by Vince Deporter
and Keith Champagne
Color by Lee Loughridge

BATMAN created by Bob Kane

SCHOLASTIC INC.
New York   Toronto   London   Auckland   Sydney
Mexico City   New Delhi   Hong Kong   Buenos Aires

ISBN 0-439-78951-6

© 2006 DC Comics
Batman and all related characters: TM & © 2006 DC Characters, Inc. All Rights Reserved.

Published by Scholastic Inc. SCHOLASTIC and associated logos
are trademarks and/or registered trademarks of Scholastic Inc.

Designed by Rick DeMonico

12 11 10 9 8 7 6 5 4 3 2 1   6 7 8 9 10/0

Printed in the U.S.A.
First printing, March 2006

An alarm shrieked in the dark streets of Gotham City. Fortunately, the city's newest protector heard the wailing siren.

The crooks quickly dumped diamonds into their bags. This was their latest in a series of jewelry store robberies. They had timed it perfectly.

One of the thieves glanced at his watch. "We have forty-five seconds before the police show up," he said. "Let's move!"

Suddenly, something crashed through the skylight above. It was Batman! He hurled his special Batarangs at the crooks.

"Forty-five seconds is all I need," said Batman. "I'll have you tied up and ready for the police!"

One of the crooks raised a gloved hand and blasted Batman with a column of ice. A wall of ice formed between Batman and the thieves.

The crooks escaped through the front door.

That's Mr. Freeze's glove, Batman thought. How did these crooks get it?

Batman paid a visit to Mr. Freeze at Arkham Asylum.

Mr. Freeze was once a small-time jewel thief named Victor Fries. After an accident, his body changed. Now he must be kept very cold to survive.

"How are you involved with the diamond burglaries?" Batman asked.

"I'm not," said Mr. Freeze. "As you can see, there's no way I can leave the safety of this Freeze Field."

Back at Wayne Manor, Bruce read an interesting article in the newspaper about the world's biggest diamond. The giant gem would be displayed at Gotham's Museum of Natural History. If the crooks were working for Mr. Freeze, they might try to steal the jewel.

"I think Batman will pay a visit to this exhibit," Bruce told his butler and friend, Alfred. "And this time, he'll dress for cold weather."

Just as Bruce suspected, the diamond thieves turned up at the museum.

The same crook used the special freeze glove to scare away the guests. Meanwhile, the other two thieves stole the giant diamond.

When Batman first fought Mr. Freeze, Alfred had developed a special snowsuit for the job. The costume was made with special insulated fabric to keep Batman warm.

It also had built-in skis so he could zip along the ice and snow.

Batman knew the suit would come in handy against his new frigid foe.

The crooks lit a fire to cover their escape. The heat from the flames made Batman very hot inside his insulated costume.

The museum's sprinkler system put out the fire, but it was too late. The thieves had escaped with the diamond!

The next day, the thieves gathered on Mount Gotham. The crooks used the large diamond to complete a giant Freeze Field projector.

When they hit the switch, the dish blasted the entire city. All of Gotham became as cold as it was in Mr. Freeze's cell.

An orderly at Arkham Asylum dropped Mr. Freeze's lunch tray. He was overcome with stiffening cold as the Freeze Field covered the city.

"I'll keep Gotham on ice until every city block pays me to turn off the Freeze Field in that section of the city," Mr. Freeze told a local news crew. "And if anyone tries to stop me, I'll flash-freeze the entire city with a flick of this switch!"

Batman had already figured out Mr. Freeze's plan. The Dark Knight strapped on his Batglider and soared toward Mount Gotham.

Batman swooped in, slicing through the freeze switch with a well-aimed Batarang. Then he threw flash capsules to distract Freeze's men.

Mr. Freeze aimed an open palm toward Batman. "Take it easy, Batman," he said with a chuckle. "Why don't you *chill out?*"

Batman retracted the wings on his Batglider so he could take down Mr. Freeze himself. Then a blast of ice slammed into him. The Caped Crusader was frozen solid.

This time, Batman was ready. He pressed a button on his Utility Belt. The tiny heating coils in his suit glowed red-hot, melting his icy prison.

Water from the melting ice dripped onto the Freeze Field projector. Sparks danced across the dish as it malfunctioned. Free from the ice, Batman landed a flying kick to the giant dish. It spun toward Mr. Freeze as it began to overload.

"No!" yelled Mr. Freeze. The dish blasted the cold criminal with all its freezing force.

Batman extended the wings of his Batglider and soared toward Gotham City. He glanced back to see several police officers arrive. They would take care of Mr. Freeze and his three thugs.

Batman smiled. "A giant ice cube is the perfect prison for someone like Mr. Freeze."